NIÑO DIABLO
SOUTH AMERICAN ROMANCES

W.H. HUDSON

British Library Cataloguing-in-Publication Data
A catalogue record for this book is available from the
British Library

William Henry Hudson

William Henry Hudson was born on 4 August 1841 in a borough of Quilmes (now Florecio Varela) in Greater Buenos Aires, Argentina. His parents, Daniel and Catherine Hudson, were American settlers of English and Irish origin. His father was a sheep farmer on a small farm in Argentina, but was sadly unsuccessful. He then turned to potato growing for a paltry existence and this led the family to near financial ruin.

Hudson spent his childhood exploring the local flora and fauna and observing the natural and human drama, on what was a lawless frontier at that time. At around fourteen or fifteen, Hudson became seriously ill with a bout of typhus, soon followed by rheumatic fever. These illnesses permanently affected his health and caused him to become more studious and contemplative. His parents obtained many books for him and his siblings to read and he occasionally had some formal education from a visiting school teacher. Charles Darwin's (1809-1882) *The Origin of Species* (1859), in particular, made a lasting impression on him.

Little is known about Hudson in the period following his parents' death. He became a wanderer, occasionally publishing his ornithological work in the *Proceedings of the Zoological Society*. He initially wrote in an English that was interlaced with Spanish idioms. He appears to have particularly loved Patagonia. Hudson immigrated to London, England in 1869, where he eventually became a British subject in 1900. In 1876 he married a much older woman and they lived precariously on the money earned from two boarding houses that she owned. She eventually inherited a house in Bayswater, London and the couple moved there.

Hudson produced a series of ornithological studies throughout his life, including *Argentine Ornithology* (1888-1899) and *British Birds* (1895). These books on ornithological studies attracted the attention of the statesman, Sir Edward Grey (1862-1933), who got Hudson a state pension in 1901. Hudson later achieved fame with his books on the English countryside, such as *Hampshire Day* (1903), *Afoot in England* (1909), and *A Shepherd's Life* (1910), which helped foster the back to nature movement of the 1920s and 1930s. His most famous fictional novel was *Green Mansions* (1904) which was an exotic romance about a traveller in the Guyana Jungle in Venezuela and his encounter with a mysterious forest girl who is half human and half bird. This romance and some of Hudson's other romances attracted the friendship of other fiction writers, such as Joseph Conrad (1857-

1924), Ford Madox Ford (1873-1939) and George Gissing (1857-1903). Hudson's most popular non-fiction novel was *Far Away and Long Ago* (1918) which recalls his childhood in Argentina. Some of his other titles include *Birds and Man* (1901), *A Little Lost Boy* (1905), *Tales of the Pampas* (1916), *Ralph Herne* (1923), and *Mary's Little Lamb* (1929).

Away from his literary work, Hudson was a founding member of the Royal Society for the Protection of Birds. Towards the end of his life he moved to Worthing, Sussex, England. He died on 18 August 1922 and is buried at Broadwater and Worthing Cemetery in Worthing where his epitaph refers to his love of birds and green places. Even after his death, Hudson had a huge legacy. In Argentina where he is known as Guillermo Enrique Hudson, his work is considered to belong to the national literature. Ernest Hemingway (1899-1961) also famously refers to Hudson's early book *The Purple Land* (1885) in his novel *The Sun Also Rises* (1926) and again to Hudson's *Far Away and Long Ago* in his posthumous novel, *The Garden of Eden* (1986). Hudson has also had two South American bird species named after him as well as a town in Berazategui Partidd and several other public places and institutions.

NIÑO DIABLO

THE wide pampa rough with long grass ; a vast level disc now growing dark, the horizon encircling it with a ring as faultless as that made by a pebble dropped into smooth water ; above it the clear sky of June, wintry and pale, still showing in the west the saffron hues of the afterglow tinged with vapoury violet and grey. In the centre of the disc a large, low rancho thatched with yellow rushes, a few stunted trees and cattle enclosures grouped about it ; and dimly seen in the shadows, cattle and sheep reposing. At the gate stands Gregory Gorostiaga, lord of house, lands and ruminating herds, leisurely unsaddling his horse ; for whatsoever Gregory does is done leisurely. Although no person is within earshot he talks much over his task, now rebuking his restive animal, and now cursing his benumbed fingers and the hard knots in his gear. A curse falls readily and not without a certain natural grace from Gregory's lips ; it is the oiled feather with which he touches every difficult knot encountered in life. From time to time he glances towards the open kitchen door, from which issue the far-flaring light of the fire and familiar voices, with savoury smells of cookery that come to his nostrils like pleasant messengers.

The unsaddling over at last the freed horse gallops away, neighing joyfully, to seek his fellows ; but Gregory is not a four-footed thing to hurry himself; and so, stepping slowly and pausing frequently to look about him as if reluctant to quit the cold night air, he turns towards the house.

The spacious kitchen was lighted by two or three wicks in cups of melted fat, and by a great fire in the middle of the clay floor that cast crowds of dancing shadows on the walls and filled the whole room with grateful warmth. On the walls were fastened many deer's heads, and on their convenient prongs were hung bridles and lassos, ropes of onions and garlics, bunches of dried herbs, and various other objects. At the fire a piece of beef was roasting on a spit; and in a large pot suspended by hook and chain from the smoke-blackened central beam, boiled and bubbled an ocean of mutton broth, puffing out white clouds of steam redolent of herbs and cummin-seed. Close to the fire, skimmer in hand, sat Magdalen, Gregory's fat and florid wife, engaged in frying pies in a second smaller pot. There also, on a high, straight-backed chair, sat Ascension, her sister-in-law, a wrinkled spinster; also, in a low rush-bottomed seat, her mother-in-law, an ancient white-headed dame, staring vacantly into the flames. On the other side of the fire were Gregory's two eldest daughters, occupied just now in serving maté to their elders—that harmless bitter decoction the sipping of which fills up all vacant moments from dawn to bed-time —pretty dove-eyed girls of sixteen, both also named Magdalen, but not after their mother nor because confusion was loved by the family for its own sake; they were twins, and born on the day sacred to Santa

Magdalena. Slumbering dogs and cats were disposed about the floor, also four children. The eldest, a boy sitting with legs outstretched before him, was cutting threads from a slip of colt's hide looped over his great toe. The two next, boy and girl, were playing a simple game called nines, once known to English children as nine men's morrice ; the lines were rudely scratched on the clay floor, and the men they played with were bits of hardened clay, nine red and as many white. The youngest, a girl of five, sat on the floor nursing a kitten that purred contentedly on her lap and drowsily winked its blue eyes at the fire and as she swayed herself from side to side she lisped out the old lullaby in her baby voice :

> *A-ro-ró mi niño*
> *A-ro-ró mi sol,*
> *A-ro-ró pedazos*
> *De mi corazon.*

Gregory stood on the threshold surveying this domestic scene with manifest pleasure.

" Papa mine, what have you brought me ? " cried the child with the kitten.

" Brought you, interested ? Stiff whiskers and cold hands to pinch your dirty little cheeks. How is your cold to-night, mother ? "

" Yes, son, it is very cold to-night ; we knew that before you came in," replied the old dame testily as she drew her chair a little closer to the fire.

" It is useless speaking to her," remarked Ascension. " With her to be out of temper is to be deaf."

" What has happened to put her out ? " he asked.

" I can tell you, papa," cried one of the twins. " She wouldn't let me make your cigars to-day, and sat down out of doors to make them herself. It was after breakfast when the sun was warm."

" And of course she fell asleep," chimed in Ascension.

" Let me tell it, auntie ! " exclaimed the other. " And she fell asleep, and in a moment Rosita's lamb came and ate up the whole of the tobacco-leaf in her lap."

" It didn't ! " cried Rosita, looking up from her game. " I opened its mouth and looked with all my eyes, and there was no tobacco-leaf in it."

" That lamb ! that lamb ! " said Gregory slily. " Is it to be wondered at that we are turning grey before our time—all except Rosita ! Remind me to-morrow, wife, to take it to the flock ; or if it has grown fat on all the tobacco-leaf, aprons and old shoes it has eaten——"

" Oh, no, no, no ! " screamed Rosita, starting up and throwing the game into confusion, just when her little brother had made a row and was in the act of seizing on one of her pieces in triumph.

" Hush, silly child, he will not harm your lamb," said the mother, pausing from her task and raising eyes that were tearful with the smoke of the fire and of the cigarette she held between her good-humoured lips. " And now, if these children have finished speaking of their important affairs, tell me, Gregory, what news do you bring ? "

" They say," he returned, sitting down and taking the maté-cup from his daughter's hand, " that the invading Indians bring seven hundred lances, and that those that first opposed them were all slain. Some say they are now retreating with the cattle they have taken; while others maintain that they are waiting to fight our men."

" Oh, my sons, my sons, what will happen to them ! " cried Magdalen, bursting into tears.

" Why do you cry, wife, before God gives you cause ? " returned her husband. " Are not all men born to fight the infidel ? Our boys are not alone—all their friends and neighbours are with them."

" Say not this to me, Gregory, for I am not a fool nor blind. All their friends indeed ! And this very day I have seen the Niño Diablo; he galloped past the house, whistling like a partridge that knows no care. Why must my two sons be called away, while he, a youth without occupation and with no mother to cry for him, remains behind ? "

" You talk folly, Magdalen," replied her lord. " Complain that the ostrich and puma are more favoured than your sons, since no man calls on them to serve the state ; but mention not the Niño, for he is freer than the wild things which Heaven has made, and fights not on this side nor on that."

" Coward ! Miserable ! " murmured the incensed mother.

Whereupon one of the twins flushed scarlet, and retorted, " He is not a coward, mother ! "

" And if not a coward why does he sit on the hearth among women and old men in times like these ? Grieved am I to hear a daughter of mine speak in defence of one who is a vagabond and a stealer of other men's horses ! "

The girl's eyes flashed angrily, but she answered not a word.

" Hold your tongue, woman, and accuse no man of crimes," spoke Gregory. " Let every Christian take proper care of his animals ; and as for the infidel's horses, he is a virtuous man that steals them. The girl speaks truth ; the Niño is no coward, but he fights not with our weapons. The web of the spider is coarse and ill-made compared with the snare he spreads to entangle his prey." Thus fixing his eyes on the face of the girl who had spoken, he added : " therefore be warned in season, my daughter, and fall not into the snare of the Niño Diablo."

Again the girl blushed and hung her head.

At this moment a clatter of hoofs, the jangling of a bell, and shouts of a traveller to the horses driven before him, came in at the open door. The dogs roused themselves, almost overturning the children in their hurry to rush out ; and up rose Gregory to find out who was approaching with so much noise.

" I know, *papita*," cried one of the children. " It is Uncle Polycarp."

" You are right, child," said her father. " Cousin Polycarp always arrives at night, shouting to his animals like a troop of Indians." And with that he went out to welcome his boisterous relative.

The traveller soon arrived, spurring his horse, scared at the light and snorting loudly, to within two yards of the door. In a few minutes the saddle was thrown off, the fore feet of the bell-mare fettered, and the horses allowed to wander away in quest of pasturage ; then the two men turned into the kitchen.

A short, burly man aged about fifty, wearing a soft hat thrust far back on his head, with truculent greenish eyes beneath arched, bushy eyebrows, and a thick shapeless nose surmounting a bristly moustache—such was Cousin Polycarp. From neck to feet he was covered with a blue cloth poncho, and on his heels he wore enormous silver spurs that clanked and jangled over the floor like the fetters of a convict. After greeting the women and bestowing the avuncular blessing on the children, who had clamoured for it as for some inestimable boon—he sat down, and flinging back his poncho displayed at his waist a huge silver-hilted knife and a heavy brass-barrelled horse-pistol.

" Heaven be praised for its goodness, Cousin Magdalen," he said. " What with pies and spices your kitchen is more fragrant than a garden of flowers. That's as it should be, for nothing but rum have I tasted this bleak day. And the boys are away fighting, Gregory tells me. Good ! When the eaglets have found out their wings let them try their talons. What, Cousin Magdalen, crying for the boys ! Would you have had them girls ? "

" Yes, a thousand times," she replied, drying her wet eyes on her apron.

" Ah, Magdalen, daughters can't be always young and sweet-tempered, like your brace of pretty partridges yonder. They grow old, Cousin Magdalen—old and ugly and spiteful ; and are more bitter and worthless than the wild pumpkin. But I speak not of those who are present, for I would say nothing to offend my respected Cousin Ascension, whom may God preserve, though she never married."

" Listen to me, Cousin Polycarp," returned the insulted dame so pointedly alluded to. " Say nothing to me nor of me, and I will also hold my peace concerning you ; for you know very well that if I were disposed to open my lips I could say a thousand things."

" Enough, enough, you have already said them a thousand times," he interrupted. " I know all that, cousin ; let us say no more."

" That is only what I ask," she retorted, " for I have never loved to bandy words with you ; and you know already, therefore I need not recall it to your mind, that if I am single it is not because some men whose names I could mention if I felt disposed—and they are the names not of dead but of living men—would not have been glad to marry me ; but because I preferred my liberty and the goods I inherited from my father ; and I see not what advantage there is in being the wife of one who is a brawler and a drunkard and spender of other people's money, and I know not what besides."

" There it is ! " said Polycarp, appealing to the fire. " I knew that I had thrust my foot into a red ants' nest— careless that I am ! But in truth, Ascension, it was fortunate for you in those distant days you mention that you hardened your heart against all lovers. For wives, like cattle that must be branded with their owner's mark, are first of all taught submission to their husbands ; and consider, cousin, what tears ! what sufferings ! " And having ended thus abruptly, he planted his elbows on his knees and busied himself with the cigarette he had been trying to roll up with his cold, drunken fingers for the last five minutes.

Ascension gave a nervous twitch at the red cotton kerchief on her head, and cleared her throat with a sound " sharp and short like the shrill swallow's cry," when——

" *Madre del Cielo*, how you frightened me ! " screamed one of the twins, giving a great start.

The cause of this sudden outcry was discovered in the presence of a young man quietly seated on the bench at the girl's side. He had not been there a minute before, and no person had seen him enter the room—what wonder that the girl was startled ! He was slender in form and had small hands and feet, and oval, olive face, smooth as a girl's except for the incipient moustache on his lip. In place of a hat he wore only a scarlet ribbon bound about his head, to keep back the glossy black hair that fell to his shoulders ; and he was wrapped in a white woollen Indian poncho, while his lower limbs were cased in white colt-skin coverings, shaped like stockings to his feet, with the red tassels of his embroidered garters falling to the ankles.

" The Niño Diablo ! " all cried in a breath, the children manifesting the greatest joy at his appearance. But old Gregory spoke with affected anger. " Why do you always drop on us in this treacherous way, like rain through a leaky thatch ? " he exclaimed. " Keep these strange arts for your visits in the infidel country ; here we are all Christians, and praise God on the threshold when we visit a neighbour's house. And now, Niño Diablo, what news of the Indians ? "

" Nothing do I know and little do I concern myself about specks on the horizon," returned the visitor with a light laugh. And at once all the children gathered round him, for the Niño they considered to belong to them when he came, and not to their elders with their solemn talk about Indian warfare and lost horses. And now, now he would finish that wonderful story, long in the telling, of the little girl alone and lost in the great desert, and surrounded by all the wild animals met to discuss what they should do with her. It was a grand story, even mother Magdalen listened, though she pretended all the time to be thinking only of her pies—and the teller, like the grand old historians of other days, put most eloquent speeches, all made out of his own head, into the lips (and beaks) of the various actors—puma, ostrich, deer, cavy, and the rest.

In the midst of this performance supper was announced, and all gathered willingly round a dish of Magdalen's pies, filled with minced meat, hard-boiled eggs chopped small, raisins, and plenty of spice. After the pies came roast beef ; and, finally, great basins of mutton broth fragrant with herbs and cummin-seed. The rage of hunger satisfied, each one said a prayer, the elders murmuring with bowed heads, the children on their knees uplifting shrill voices. Then followed the concluding semi-religious ceremony of the day, when each child in its turn asked a blessing of father, mother, grandmother, uncle, aunt, and not omitting the stranger within the gates, even the Niño Diablo of evil-sounding name.

The men drew forth their pouches, and began makiɪ g

their cigarettes, when once more the children gathered round the story-teller, their faces glowing with expectation.

" No, no," cried their mother. " No more stories to-night—to bed, to bed ! "

" Oh, mother, mother ! " cried Rosita pleadingly, and struggling to free herself; for the good woman had dashed in among them to enforce obedience. " Oh, let me stay till the story ends ! The reed-cat has said such things ! Oh, what will they do with the poor little girl ? "

" And oh, mother mine ! " drowsily sobbed her little sister; " the armadillo that said—that said nothing because it had nothing to say, and the partridge that whistled and said—" and here she broke into a prolonged wail. The boys also added their voices until the hubbub was no longer to be borne, and Gregory rose up in his wrath and called on some one to lend him a big whip; only then they yielded, and still sobbing and casting many a lingering look behind, were led from the kitchen.

During this scene the Niño had been carrying on a whispered conversation with the pretty Magdalen of his choice, heedless of the uproar of which he had been the indirect cause; deaf also to the bitter remarks of Ascension concerning some people who, having no homes of their own, were fond of coming uninvited into other people's houses, only to repay the hospitality extended to them by stealing their silly daughters' affections, and teaching their children to rebel against their authority.

But the noise and confusion had served to arouse Poly-carp from a drowsy fit; for like a boa constrictor, he had dined largely after his long fast, and dinner had made him

dull ; bending towards his cousin he whispered earnestly :
" Who is this young stranger, Gregory ? "

" In what corner of the earth have you been hiding to
ask who the Niño Diablo is ? " returned the other.

" Must I know the history of every cat and dog ? "

" The Niño is not cat nor dog, cousin, but a man among
men, like a falcon among birds. When a child of six the
Indians killed all his relations and carried him into
captivity. After five years he escaped out of their hands,
and, guided by sun and stars and signs on the earth, he
found his way back to the Christians' country, bringing
many beautiful horses stolen from his captors ; also the
name of Niño Diablo first given to him by the infidel.
We know him by no other."

" This is a good story ; in truth I like it well—it pleases
me mightily," said Polycarp. " And what more, cousin
Gregory ? "

" More than I can tell, cousin. When he comes the dogs
bark not—who knows why? His tread is softer than the
cat's ; the untamed horse is tame for him. Always in the
midst of dangers, yet no harm, no scratch. Why?
Because he stoops like the falcon, makes his stroke and is
gone—Heaven knows where ! "

" What strange things are you telling me ? Wonderful !
And what more, cousin Gregory ? "

" He often goes into the Indian country, and lives freely
with the infidel, disguised, for they do not know him who
was once their captive. They speak of the Niño Diablo
to him, saying that when they catch that thief they will
flay him alive. He listens to their strange stories, then

leaves them, taking their finest ponchos and silver orna-
ments, and the flower of their horses."

"A brave youth, one after my own heart, cousin
Gregory. Heaven defend and prosper him in all his
journeys into the Indian territory ! Before we part I shall
embrace him and offer him my friendship, which is worth
something. More, tell me more, cousin Gregory ? "

" These things I tell you to put you on your guard ; look
well to your horses, cousin."

" What ! " shouted the other, lifting himself up from his
stooping posture, and staring at his relation with astonish
ment and kindling anger in his countenance.

The conversation had been carried on in a low tone,
and the sudden loud exclamation startled them all—all
except the Niño, who continued smoking and chatting
pleasantly to the twins.

" Lightning and pestilence, what is this you say to me,
Gregory Gorostiaga ! " continued Polycarp, violently
slapping his thigh and thrusting his hat farther back on
his head.

" Prudence ! " whispered Gregory. " Say nothing to
offend the Niño; he never forgives an enemy—with
horses."

" Talk not to me of prudence ! " bawled the other.
You hit me on the apple of the eye and counsel me not to
cry out. What ! have not I, whom men call Polycarp of
the South, wrestled with tigers in the desert, and must I
hold my peace because of a boy—even a boy devil ? Talk
of what you like, cousin, and I am a meek man—meek as
a sucking babe ; but touch not on my horses, for then I am

AA

a whirlwind, a conflagration, a river flooded in winter, and all wrath and destruction like an invasion of Indians ! Who can stand before me ? Ribs of steel are no protection ! Look at my knife ; do you ask why there are stains on the blade ? Listen ; because it has gone straight to the robber's heart ! " And with that he drew out his great knife and flourished it wildly, and made stabs and slashes at an imaginary foe suspended above the fire.

The pretty girls grew silent and pale and trembled like poplar leaves ; the old grandmother rose up, and clutching at her shawl toddled hurriedly away, while Ascension uttered a snort of disdain. But the Niño still talked and smiled, blowing thin smoke-clouds from his lips, careless of the tempest of wrath gathering before him ; till, seeing the other so calm, the man of war returned his weapon to its sheath, and glancing round and lowering his voice to a conversational tone, informed his hearers that his name was Polycarp, one known and feared by all men,—especially in the south ; that he was disposed to live in peace and amity with the entire human race, and he therefore considered it unreasonable of some men to follow him about the world asking him to kill them. " Perhaps," he concluded, with a touch of irony, " they think I gain something by putting them to death. A mistake, good friends ; I gain nothing by it ! I am not a vulture, and their dead bodies can be of no use to me."

Just after this sanguinary protest and disclaimer the Niño all at once made a gesture as if to impose silence, and turning his face towards the door, his nostrils dilating, and his eyes appearing to grow large and luminous like those of a cat.

NIÑO DIABLO

" What do you hear, Niño ? " asked Gregory.

" I hear lapwings screaming," he replied.

" Only at a fox perhaps," said the other. " But go to the door, Niño, and listen."

" No need," he returned, dropping his hand, the light of a sudden excitement passing from his face. " 'Tis only a single horseman riding this way at a fast gallop."

Polycarp got up and went to the door, saying that when a man was among robbers it behoved him to look well after his cattle. Then he came back and sat down again. " Perhaps," he remarked, with a side glance at the Niño, " a better plan would be to watch the thief. A lie, cousin Gregory ; no lapwings are screaming ; no single horseman approaching at a fast gallop. The night is serene, and earth as silent as the sepulchre."

" Prudence ! " whispered Gregory again. " Ah, cousin, always playful like a kitten ; when will you grow old and wise ? Can you not see a sleeping snake without turning aside to stir it up with your naked foot ? "

Strange to say, Polycarp made no reply. A long experience in getting up quarrels had taught him that these impassive men were, in truth, often enough like venomous snakes, quick and deadly when roused. He became secret and watchful in his manner.

All now were intently listening. Then said Gregory, " Tell us, Niño, what voices, fine as the trumpet of the smallest fly, do you hear coming from that great silence ? Has the mother skunk put her little ones to sleep in their kennel and gone out to seek for the pipit's nest ? Have fox and armadillo met to challenge each other to fresh trials of strength and cunning? What is the owl saying this moment to his mistress in praise of her big, green eyes?"

The young man smiled slightly, but answered not; and for full five minutes more all listened, then sounds of approaching hoofs became audible. Dogs began to bark, horses to snort in alarm, and Gregory rose and went forth to receive the late night-wanderer. Soon he appeared, beating the angry barking dogs off with his whip, a white-faced, wild-haired man, furiously spurring his horse like a person demented or flying from robbers.

"*Ave Maria!*" he shouted aloud; and when the answer was given in suitable pious words, the scared-looking stranger drew near and bending down said, "Tell me, good friend, is one whom men call Niño Diablo with you; for to this house I have been directed in my search for him?"

"He is within, friend," answered Gregory. "Follow me and you shall see him with your own eyes. Only first unsaddle, so that your horse may roll before the sweat dries on him."

"How many horses have I ridden their last journey on this quest!" said the stranger, hurriedly pulling off the saddle and rugs. "But tell me one thing more; is he well —no indisposition? Has he met with no accident—a broken bone, a sprained ankle?"

"Friend," said Gregory, "I have heard that once in past times the moon met with an accident, but of the Niño no such thing has been reported to me."

With this assurance the stranger followed his host

into the kitchen, made his salutation, and sat down by the fire. He was about thirty years old, a good-looking man, but his face was haggard, his eyes bloodshot, his manner restless, and he appeared like one half-crazed by some great calamity. The hospitable Magdalen placed food before him and pressed him to eat. He complied, although reluctantly, despatched his supper in a few moments, and murmured a prayer ; then, glancing curiously at the two men seated near him, he addressed himself to the burly, well-armed, and dangerous-looking Polycarp. " Friend," he said, his agitation increasing as he spoke, " four days have I been seeking you, taking neither food nor rest, so great was my need of your assistance. You alone, after God, can help me. Help me in this strait, and half of all I possess in land and cattle and gold shall be freely given to you, and the angels above will applaud your deed ! "

" Drunk or mad ? " was the reply vouchsafed to this appeal.

" Sir," said the stranger with dignity, " I have not tasted wine these many days, nor has my great grief crazed me."

" Then what ails the man ? " said Polycarp. " Fear perhaps, for he is white in the face like one who has seen the Indians."

" In truth I have seen them. I was one of those unfortunates who first opposed them, and most of the friends who were with me are now food for wild dogs. Where our houses stood there are only ashes and a stain of blood on the ground. " Oh friend, can you not guess why you alone were in my thought when this trouble came to me—why I have ridden day and night to find you ? "

" Demons ! " exclaimed Polycarp, " into what quag-mires would this man lead me ? Once for all I under-stand you not ! Leave me in peace, strange man, or we shall quarrel." And here he tapped his weapon significantly.

At this juncture, Gregory, who took his time about everything, thought proper to interpose. " You are mistaken, friend," said he. " The young man sitting on your right is the Niño Diablo, for whom you inquired a little while ago."

A look of astonishment, followed by one of intense relief, came over the stranger's face. Turning to the young man he said, " My friend, forgive me this mistake. Grief has perhaps dimmed my sight ; but sometimes the iron blade and the blade of finest temper are not easily distinguished by the eye. When we try them we know which is the brute metal, and cast it aside to take up the other, and trust our life to it. The words I have spoken were meant for you, and you have heard them."

" What can I do for you, friend ? " said the Niño.

" Oh, sir, the greatest service ! You can restore my lost wife to me. The savages have taken her away into captivity. What can I do to save her—I who cannot make myself invisible, and fly like the wind, and compass all things ! " And here he bowed his head, and covering his face gave way to over-mastering grief.

" Be comforted, friend," said the other, touching him lightly on the arm. " I will restore her to you."

" Oh, friend, how shall I thank you for these words ! "

cried the unhappy man, seizing and pressing the Niño's hand.

" Tell me her name—describe her to me."

" Torcuata is her name—Torcuata de la Rosa. She is one finger's width taller than this young woman," indicating one of the twins who was standing. " But not dark ; her cheeks are rosy—no, no, I forget, they will be pale now, whiter than the grass plumes, with stains of dark colour under the eyes. Brown hair and blue eyes, but very deep blue. Look well, friend, lest you think them black and leave her to perish."

" Never ! " remarked Gregory, shaking his head.

" Enough—you have told me enough, friend," said the Niño, rolling up a cigarette.

" Enough ! " repeated the other, surprised. " But you do not know ; she is my life ; my life is in your hands. How can I persuade you to be with me. Cattle I have. I had gone to pay the herdsmen their wages when the Indians came unexpectedly ; and my house at La Chilca on the banks of the Langueyú, was burnt, and my wife taken away during my absence. Eight hundred head of cattle have escaped the savages, and half of them shall be yours ; and half of all I possess in money and land."

" Cattle ! " returned the Niño, smiling, and holding a lighted stick to his cigarette. " I have enough to eat without molesting myself with the care of cattle."

" But I told you that I had other things," said the stranger, full of distress.

The young man laughed, and rose from his seat.

" Listen to me," he said. " I go now to follow the

Indians—to mix with them, perhaps. They are retreating slowly, burdened with much spoil. In fifteen days go to the little town of Tandil, and wait for me there. As for land, if God has given so much of it to the ostrich it is not a thing for a man to set a great value on." Then he bent down to whisper a few words in the ear of the girl at his side; and immediately afterwards, with a simple " good-night " to the others, stepped lightly from the kitchen. By another door the girl also hurriedly left the room, to hide her tears from the watchful censuring eyes of mother and aunt.

Then the stranger, recovering from his astonishment at the abrupt ending of the conversation, started up, and crying aloud, " Stay ! stay one moment—one word more ! " rushed out after the young man. At some distance from the house he caught sight of the Niño, sitting motionless on his horse, as if waiting to speak to him.

" This is what I have to say to you," spoke the Niño, bending down to the other. " Go back to Langueyú, and rebuild your house, and expect me there with your wife in about thirty days. When I bade you go to the Tandil in fifteen days, I spoke only to mislead that man Polycarp, who has an evil mind. Can I ride a hundred leagues and back in fifteen days ? Say no word of this to any man. And fear not. If I fail to return with your wife at the appointed time take some of that money you have offered me, and bid a priest say a mass for my soul's repose; for eye of man shall never see me again, and the brown hawks will be complaining that there is no more flesh to be picked from my bones."

During this brief colloquy, and afterwards, when Gregory and his women-folk went off to bed, leaving the stranger to sleep in his rugs beside the kitchen fire, Polycarp, who had sworn a mighty oath not to close his eyes that night, busied himself making his horses secure. Driving them home, he tied them to the posts of the gate within twenty-five yards of the kitchen door. Then he sat down by the fire and smoked and dozed, and cursed his dry mouth and drowsy eyes that were so hard to keep open. At intervals of about fifteen minutes he would get up and go out to satisfy himself that his precious horses were still safe. At length in rising, some time after midnight, his foot kicked against some loud-sounding metal object lying beside him on the floor, which on examination proved to be a copper bell of a peculiar shape, and curiously like the one fastened to the neck of his bellmare. Bell in hand, he stepped to the door and put out his head, and lo ! his horses were no longer at the gate ! Eight horses : seven iron-grey geldings, every one of them swift and sure-footed, sound as the bell in his hand, and as like each other as seven claret-coloured eggs in the tinamou's nest ; and the eighth the gentle piebald mare— the *madrina* his horses loved and would follow to the world's end, now, alas ! with a thief on her back ! Gone —gone !

He rushed out, uttering a succession of frantic howls and imprecations ; and finally, to wind up the performance, dashed the now useless bell with all his energy against the gate, shattering it into a hundred pieces. Oh, that bell, how often and how often in how many a wayside public-house had he boasted, in his cups and when sober, of its mellow, far-reaching tone,—the sweet sound that assured him in the silent watches of the night that his beloved steeds were safe! Now he danced on the broken fragments, digging them into the earth with his heel; now in his frenzy, he could have dug them up again to grind them to powder with his teeth!

The children turned restlessly in bed, dreaming of the lost little girl in the desert; and the stranger half awoke, muttering, " Courage, O Torcuata—let not your heart break. . . . Soul of my life, he gives you back to me—on my bosom, *rosa fresca, rosa fresca!*" Then the hands unclenched themselves again, and the muttering died away. But Gregory woke fully, and instantly divined the cause of the clamour. "Magdalen! Wife!" he said. "Listen to Polycarp; the Niño has paid him out for his insolence! Oh, fool, I warned him, and he would not listen!" But Magdalen refused to wake; and so, hiding his head under the coverlet, he made the bed shake with suppressed laughter, so pleased was he at the clever trick played on his blustering cousin. All at once his laughter ceased, and out popped his head again, showing in the dim light a somewhat long and solemn face. For he had suddenly thought of his pretty daughter asleep in the adjoining room. Asleep! Wide awake, more likely, thinking of her sweet lover, brushing the dew from the hoary pampas grass in his southward flight, speeding away into the heart of the vast mysterious wilderness. Listening also to her uncle, the desperado, apostrophizing the midnight stars; while with his knife he excavates two deep trenches, three yards long and intersecting each other at right angles—a sacred symbol on which he intends, when finished, to swear a most horrible vengeance. "Perhaps," muttered Gregory, "the Niño has still other prânks to play in this house."

When the stranger heard next morning what had happened, he was better able to understand the Niño's motive in giving him that caution overnight; nor was he greatly put out, but thought it better that an evil-minded man should lose his horses than that the Niño should set out badly mounted on such an adventure.

"Let me not forget," said the robbed man, as he rode away on a horse borrowed from his cousin, "to be at the Tandil this day fortnight, with a sharp knife and a blunderbuss charged with a handful of powder and not fewer than twenty-three slugs."

Terribly in earnest was Polycarp of the South! He was there at the appointed time, slugs and all; but the smooth-cheeked, mysterious, child-devil came not; nor, stranger still, did the scared-looking de la Rosa come clattering in to look for his lost Torcuata. At the end of the fifteenth day de la Rosa was at Langueyú, seventy-five miles from the Tandil, alone in his new rancho, which had just been rebuilt with the aid of a few neighbours. Through all that night he sat alone by the fire, pondering many things. If he could only recover his lost wife, then he would bid a long farewell to that wild frontier and take her across the great sea, and to that old tree-shaded stone farm-house in Andalusia, which he had left a boy, and where his aged parents still lived, thinking no more to see their wandering son. His resolution was taken; he would sell all he possessed, all except a portion of land in the Langueyú with the house he had just rebuilt; and to the Niño Diablo, the deliverer, he would say, " Friend, though you despise the things that others value, take this land and poor house for the sake of the girl Magdalen you love; for then perhaps her parents will no longer deny her to you."

He was still thinking of these things, when a dozen or twenty military starlings—that cheerful scarlet-breasted songster of the lonely pampas—alighted on the thatch outside, and warbling their gay, careless winter-music told him that it was day. And all day long, on foot and on horseback, his thoughts were of his lost Torcuata; and when evening once more drew near his heart was sick with suspense and longing; and climbing the ladder placed against the gable of his rancho he stood on the roof gazing westwards into the blue distance. The sun, crimson and large, sunk into the great green sea of grass, and from all the plain rose the tender fluting notes of the tinamou-partridges, bird answering bird. " Oh, that I could pierce the haze with my vision," he murmured, " that I could see across a hundred leagues of level plain, and look this moment on your sweet face, Torcuata ! "

And Torcuata was in truth a hundred leagues distant from him at that moment; and if the miraculous sight he wished for had been given, this was what he would have seen. A wide, barren plain scantily clothed with yellow tufts of grass and thorny shrubs, and at its southern extremity, shutting out the view on that side, a low range of dune-like hills. Over this level ground, towards the range, moves a vast herd of cattle and horses—fifteen or twenty thousand head—followed by a scattered horde of savages armed with their long lances. In a small compact body in the centre ride the captives, women and children. Just as the red orb touches the horizon the hills are passed, and lo! a wide, grassy valley beyond, with flocks and herds pasturing, and scattered trees, and the blue gleam of water from a chain of small lakes! There full in sight is the Indian settlement, the smoke rising peacefully up from the clustered huts. At the sight of home the savages burst into loud cries of joy and triumph, answered, as they drew near, with piercing screams of welcome from the village population, chiefly composed of women, children and old men.

It is past midnight; the young moon has set; the last fires are dying down; the shouts and loud noise of excited talk and laughter have ceased, and the weary warriors, after feasting on sweet mare's flesh to repletion, have fallen asleep in their huts, or lying out of doors on the ground. Only the dogs are excited still and keep up an incessant barking. Even the captive women, huddled together in one hut in the middle of the settlement, fatigued with their long rough journey, have cried themselves to sleep at last.

At length one of the sad sleepers wakes, or half wakes, dreaming that someone has called her name. How could such a thing be? Yet her own name still seems ringing in her brain, and at length, fully awake, she finds herself intently listening. Again it sounded—" Torcuata "—a voice fine as the pipe of a mosquito, yet so sharp and distinct that it tingled in her ear. She sat up and listened again, and once more it sounded " Torcuata ! " " Who speaks ? " she returned in a fearful whisper. The voice, still fine and small, replied, " Come out from among the others until you touch the wall." Trembling she obeyed, creeping out from among the sleepers until she came into contact with the side of the hut. Then the voice sounded again, " Creep round the wall until you come to a small crack of light on the other side." Again she obeyed, and when she reached the line of faint light it widened quickly to an aperture, through which a shadowy arm was passed round her waist ; and in a moment she was lifted up, and saw the stars above her, and at her feet dark forms of men wrapped in their ponchos lying asleep. But no one woke, no alarm was given ; and in a very few minutes she was mounted, man-fashion, on a bare-backed horse, speeding swiftly over the dim plains, with the shadowy form of her mysterious deliverer some yards in advance, driving before him a score or so of horses. He had only spoken half-a-dozen words to her since their escape from the hut, but she knew by those words that he was taking her to Langueyú.

.